Learn to Draw

FOREST ANIMALS

Learn to draw 10 forest animals in easy to follow steps

Learn to Draw: **Rabbit**

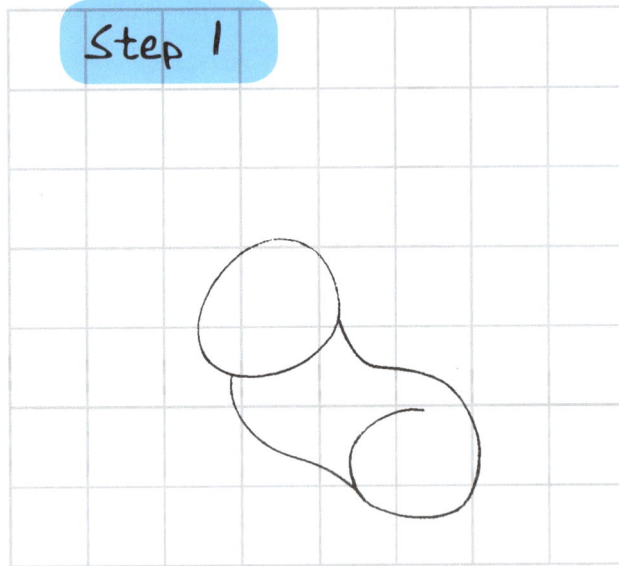

Draw an egg shape for the head.
Draw the body as shown.

Draw two long ears. Add a little nose to
the front of the face.

Draw two front legs and two hind
legs. Add a fluffy tail.

Give the rabbit an eye, whiskers
and smile. Add detail to the ears.

Place the Sticker

Colour
like this

Time to Draw...

Learn to Draw: **Beaver**

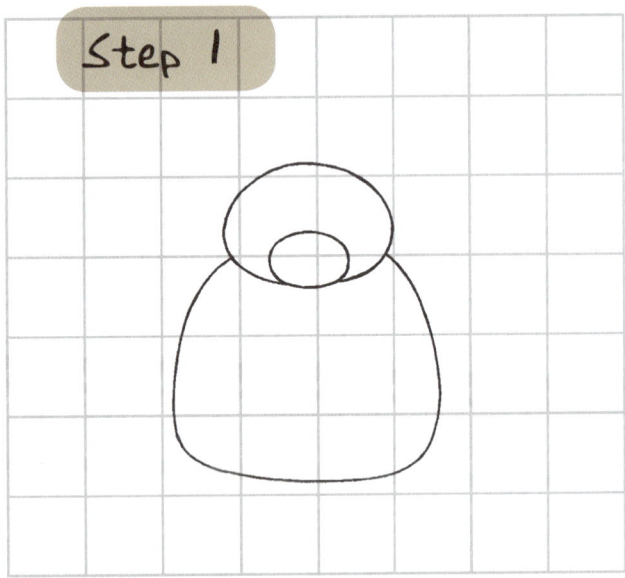

Step 1

Draw two ovals, one for the head and one for the nose. Add a body.

Step 2

Draw ears and feet. Add an inner oval for the tummy and a tooth.

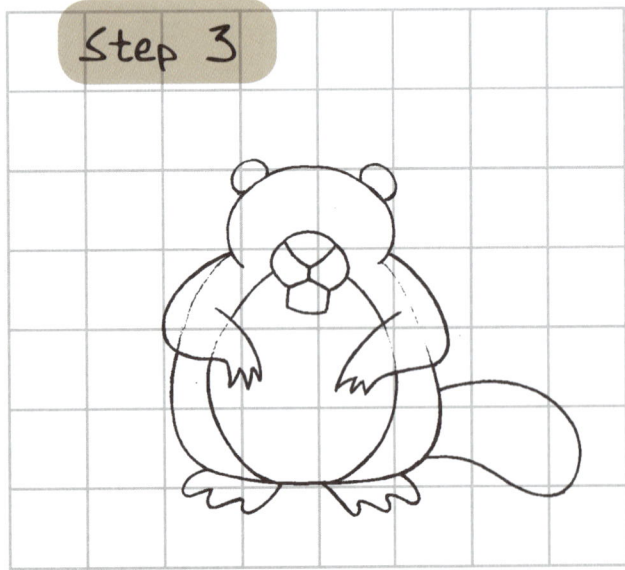

Step 3

Draw a long thick tail and two arms. Add detail to the nose.

Step 4

Give the beaver eyes, whiskers and two teeth. Add detail to the tail.

Place the Sticker

Drawing Tips
Try not to rest your hand on the paper while drawing. This will avoid making smudges and marks.

Colour
like
this

Time to Draw...

Learn to Draw: Deer

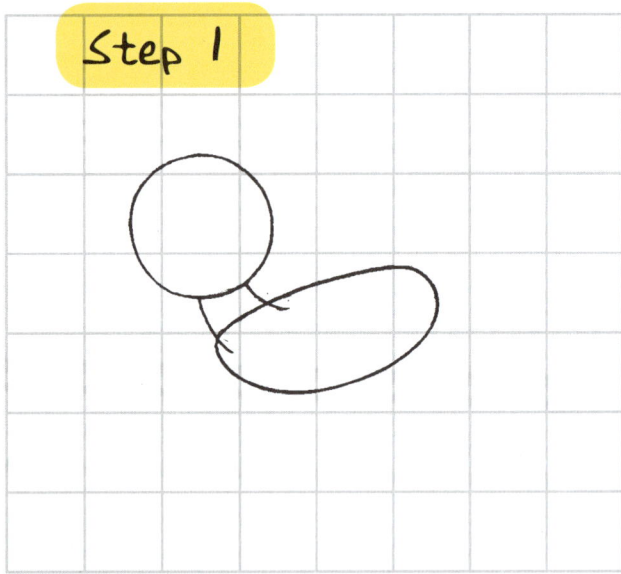

Draw a circle for the head. Add a bean shape for the body.

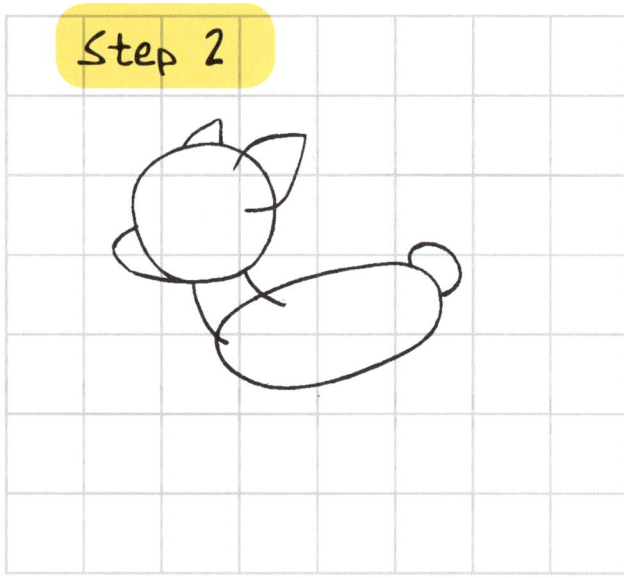

Draw a little tail and a nose. Add two ears.

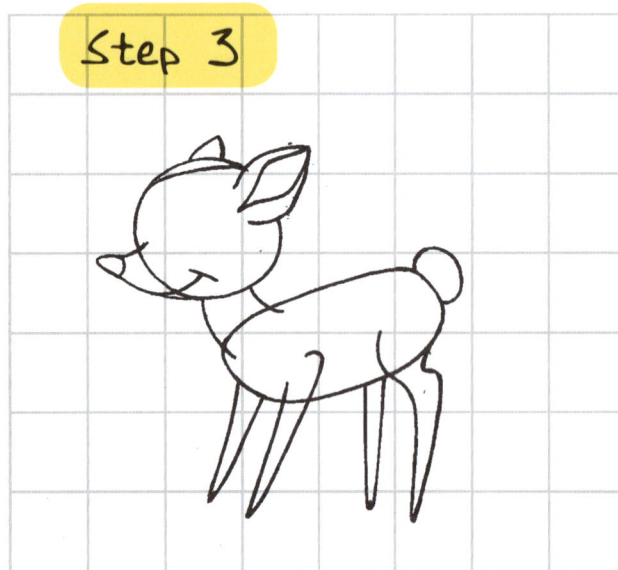

Draw four legs as shown. Add detail to nose and ears.

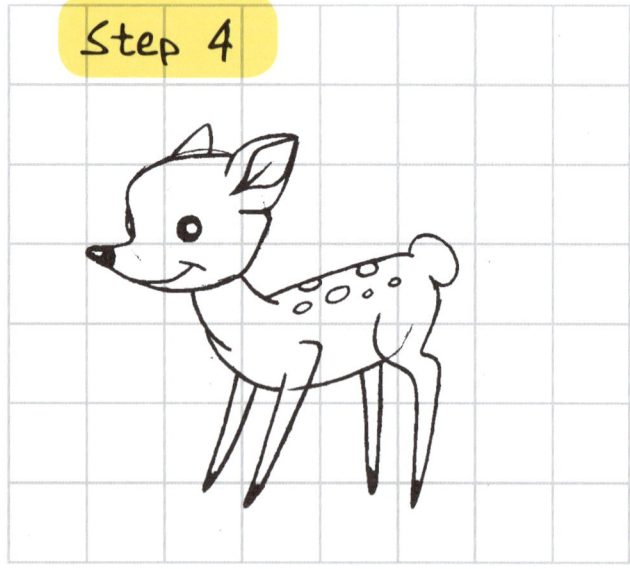

Give the deer eyes and a smile. Add feet and body detail as shown.

Place the Sticker

Drawing Tips
Keep your hard pencils sharp and soft pencils blunt. They can be used for outlines and shading respectively.

Colour like this

Time to Draw...

Learn to Draw: **Brown Bear**

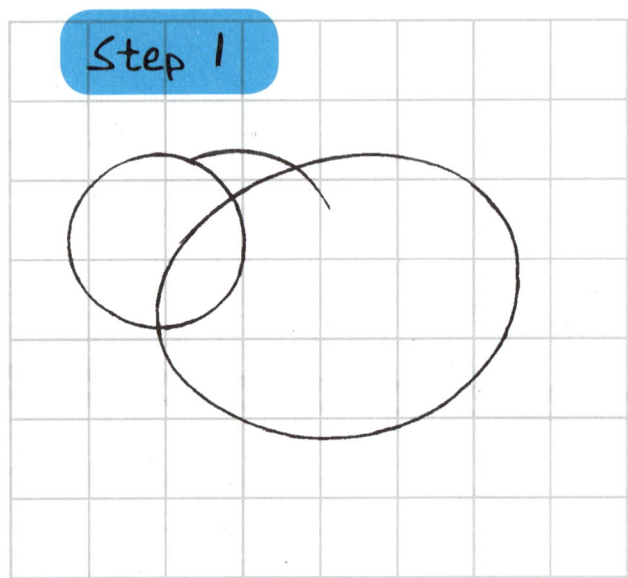

Step 1

Draw a large oval for the body and a circle for the head.

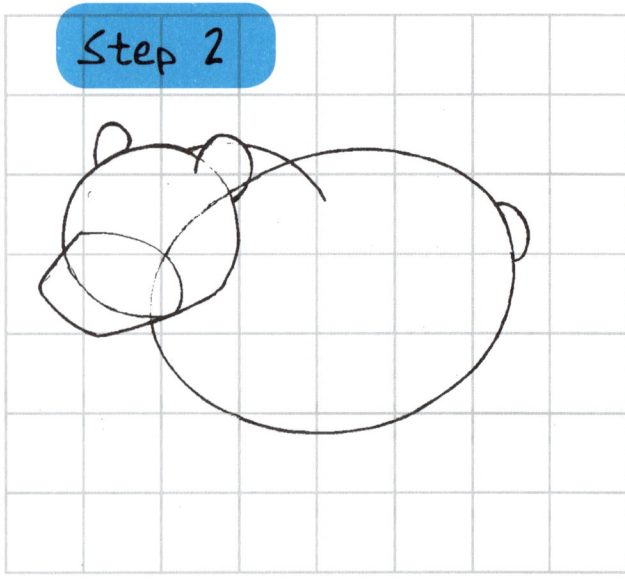

Step 2

Draw the tail and the nose. Add two little ears.

Step 3

Draw four legs as shown. Add a round nose.

Step 4

Give the bear eyes and small whiskers. Add detail to the feet and ears.

Place the Sticker

Colour
like this

Time to Draw...

Learn to Draw: **Wolf**

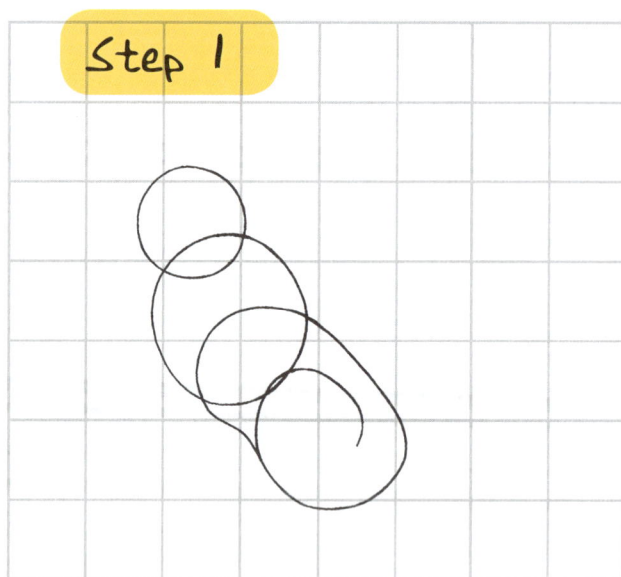

Step 1

Draw a circle shape for the head. Add the rest of the body as shown.

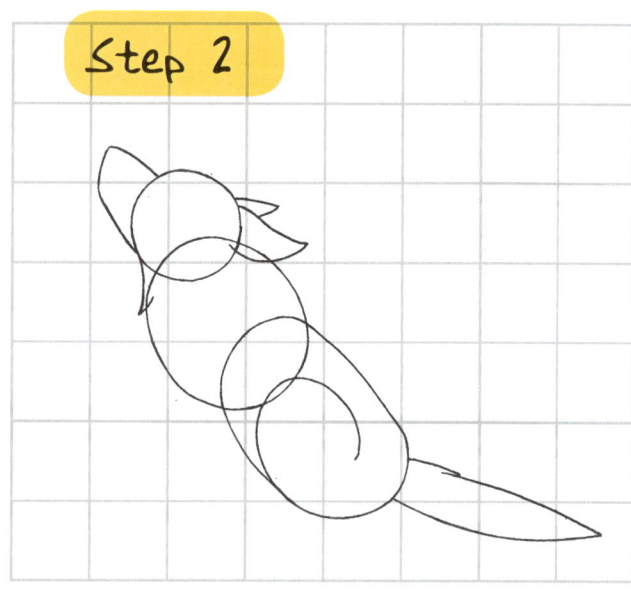

Step 2

Draw a long nose and two pointy ears. Add a long tail.

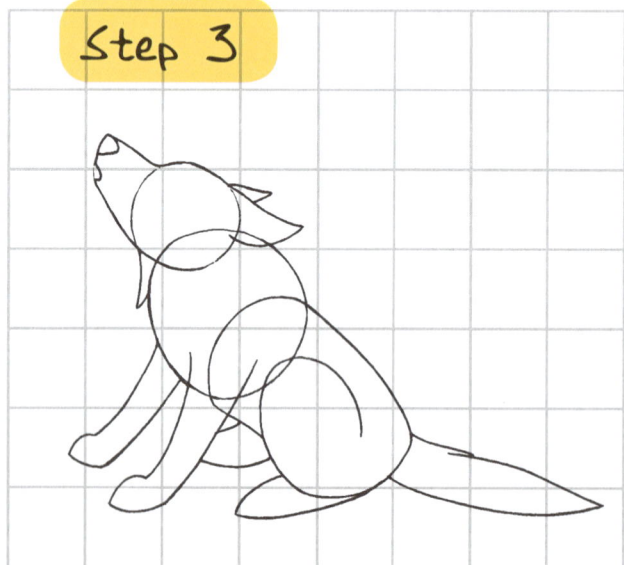

Step 3

Draw four legs as shown. Add a little nose and mouth.

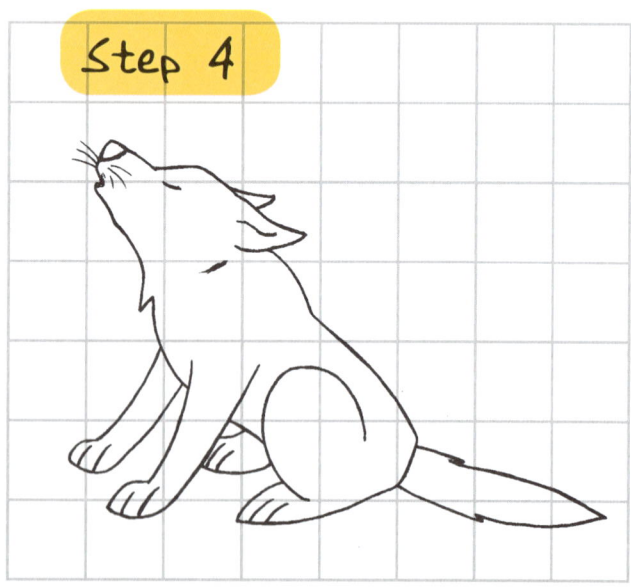

Step 4

Give the wolf an eye and whiskers. Add detail to the feet and fur.

Place the Sticker

Colour
like
this

Time to Draw...

Learn to Draw: Hedgehog

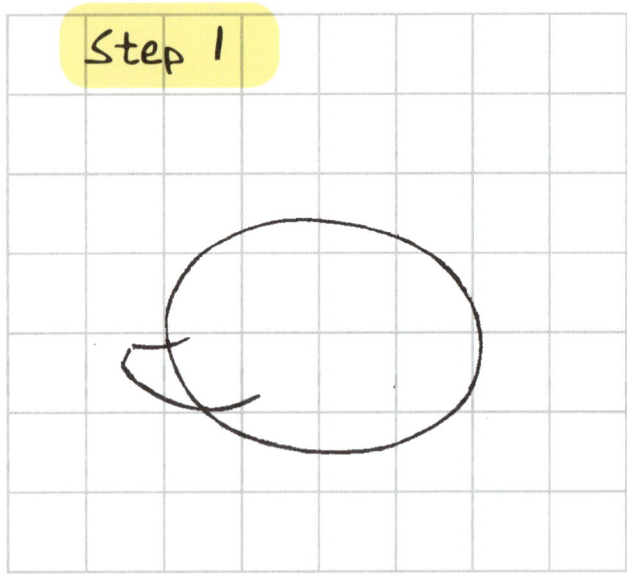

Step 1

Draw an oval shape for the body and add a nose.

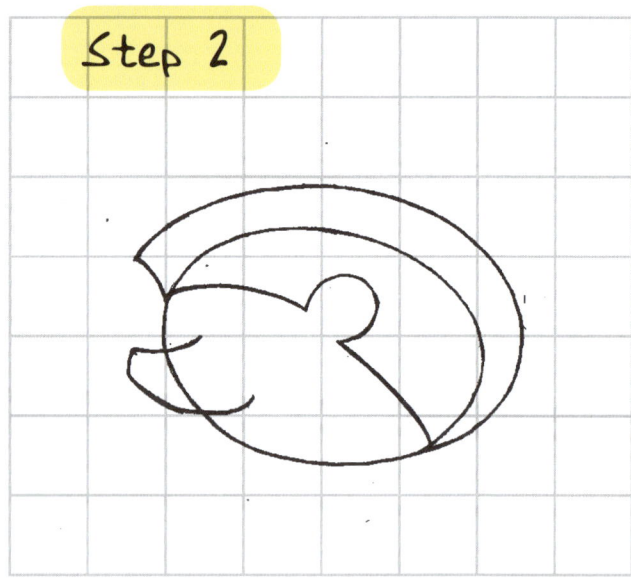

Step 2

Draw the ear shape and the rough outline for the spikes.

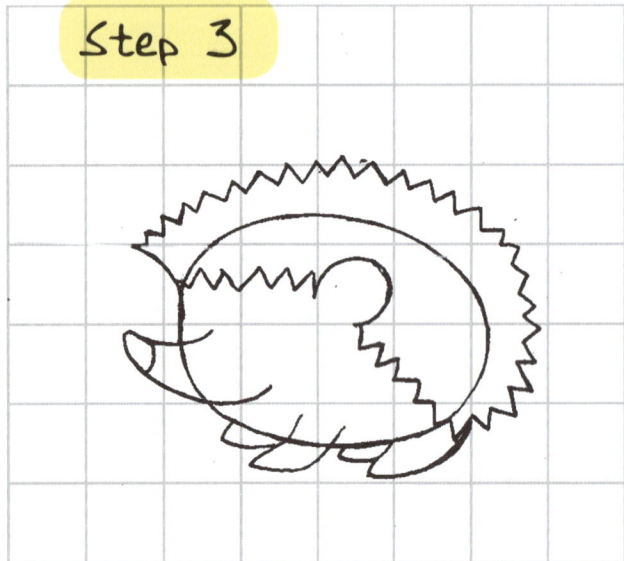

Step 3

Draw four little feet. Add spikes to the body as shown.

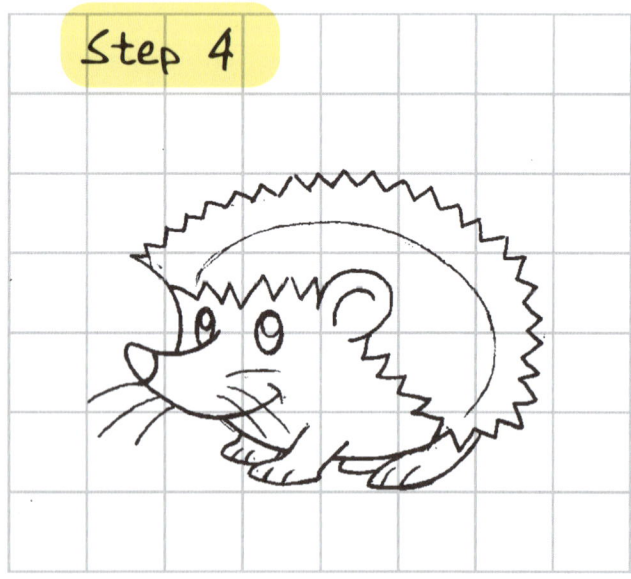

Step 4

Give the hedgehog eyes, a smile and whiskers. Add detail to the feet.

Place the Sticker

Colour
like
this

Time to Draw...

Learn to Draw: Badger

Step 1

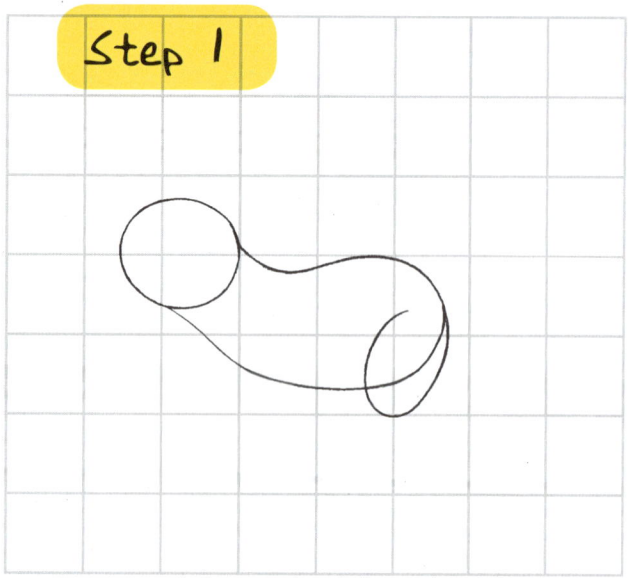

Draw a circle shape for the head. Add the body as shown.

Step 2

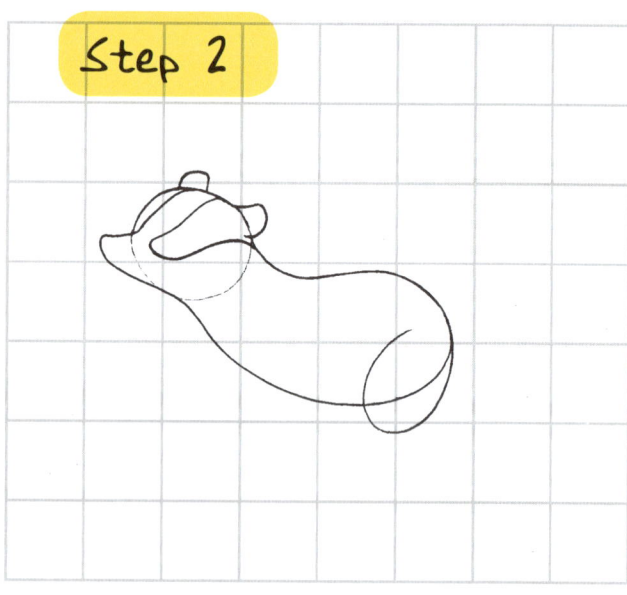

Draw a nose and two ears. Add detail to the face as shown.

Step 3

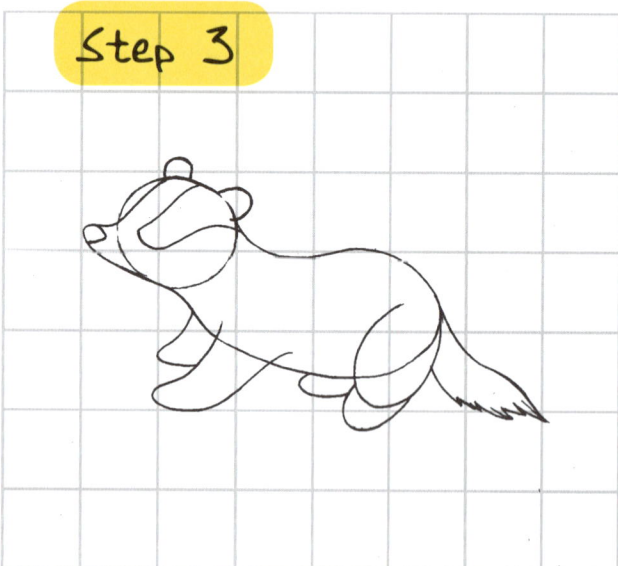

Draw two front legs and two hind legs as shown. Add a tail.

Step 4

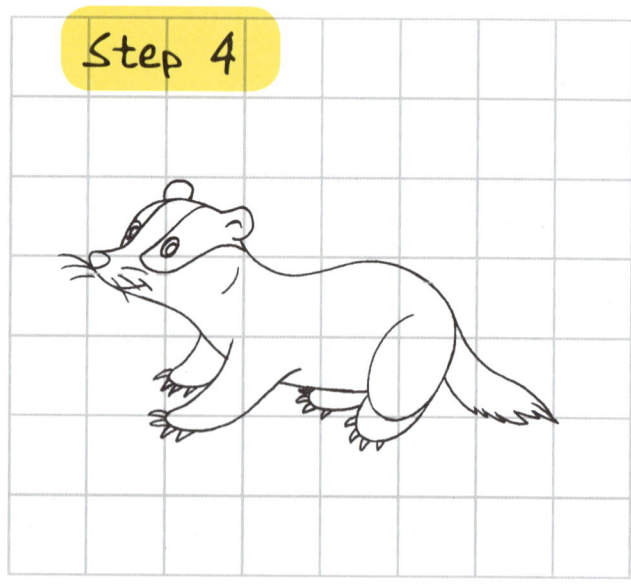

Give the badger eyes, a nose and whiskers. Add claws to his feet.

Place the Sticker

Colour like this

Time to Draw...

Learn to Draw: Squirrel

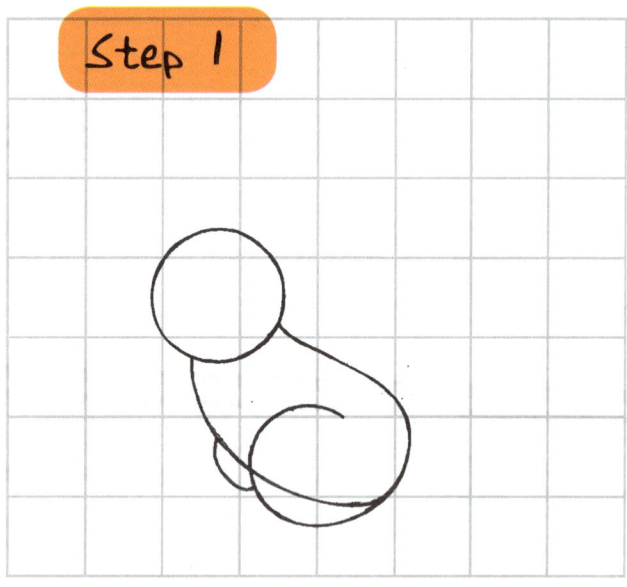

Step 1

Draw a circle shape for the head. Add the body as shown.

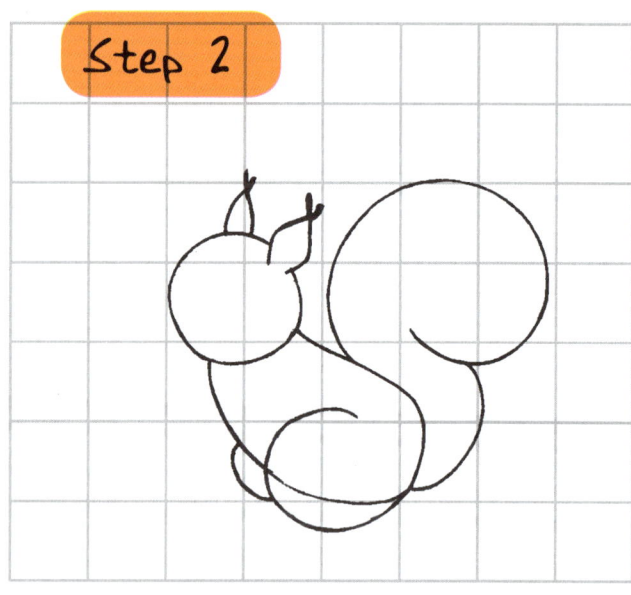

Step 2

Draw a big bushy tail. Add two pointy ears.

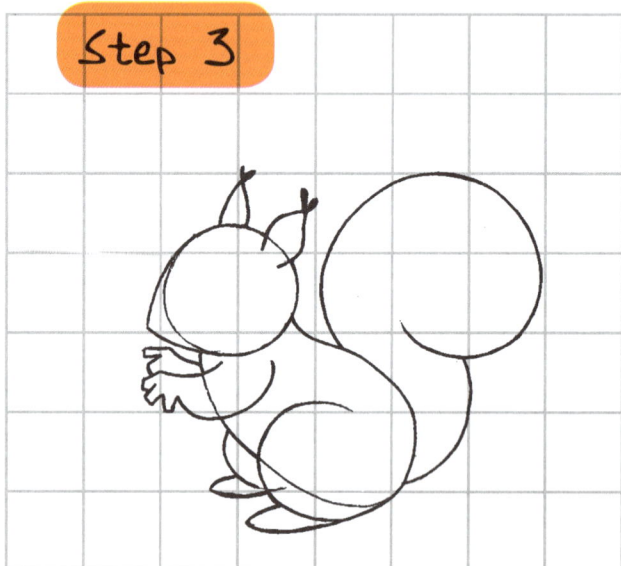

Step 3

Draw two little feet and two arms as shown. Add a nose.

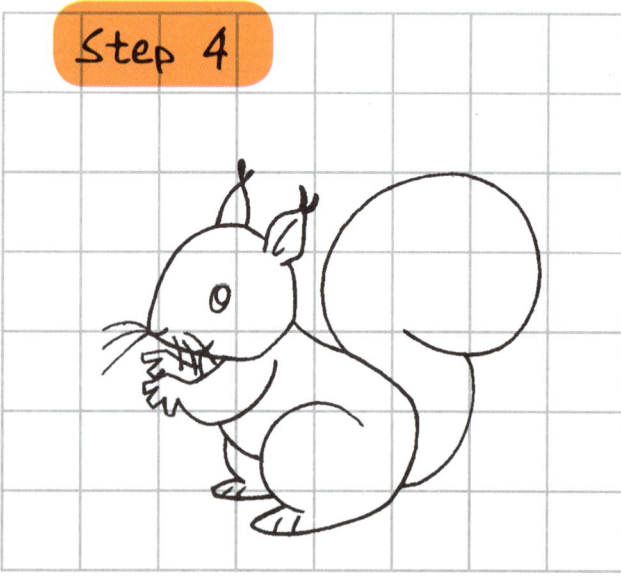

Step 4

Give the squirrel a nose, eye and whiskers. Add detail to the feet.

Place the Sticker

Colour like this

Time to Draw...

Learn to Draw: **Owl**

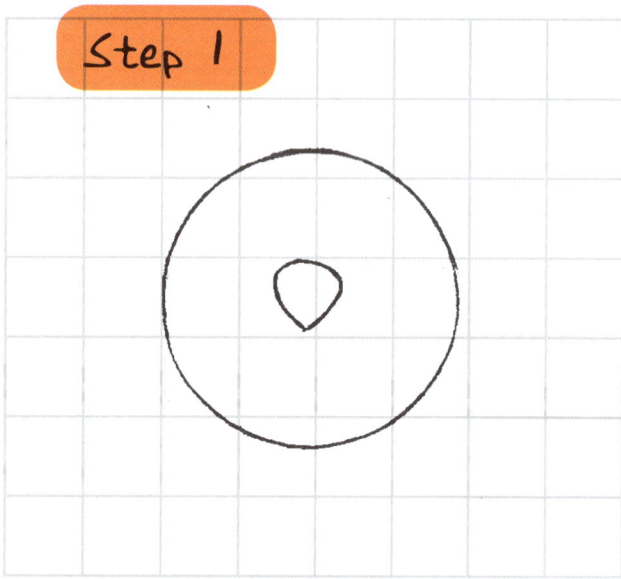

Draw a large circle for the owl's body. Add a little beak.

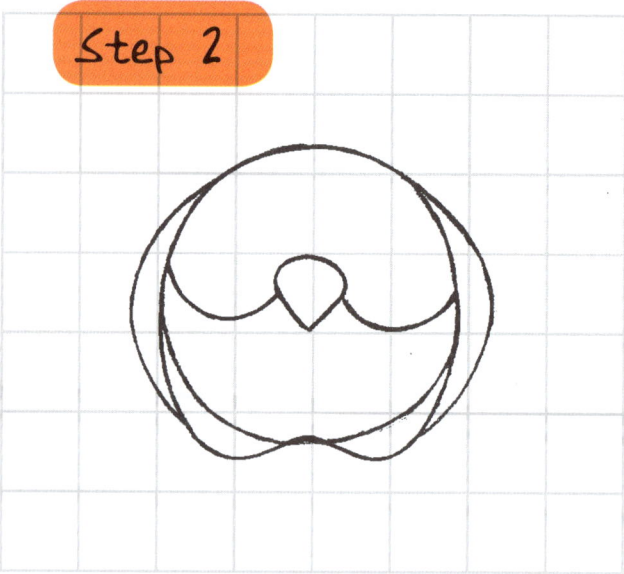

Draw a wing either side of the body. Add detail to the face as shown.

Draw two little feet, two circles for the eyes and two tufts of feathers.

Give the owl some eyes. Add feather detail to the body and add a branch.

Place the Sticker

Colour like this

Time to Draw...

Learn to Draw: **Fox**

Step 1

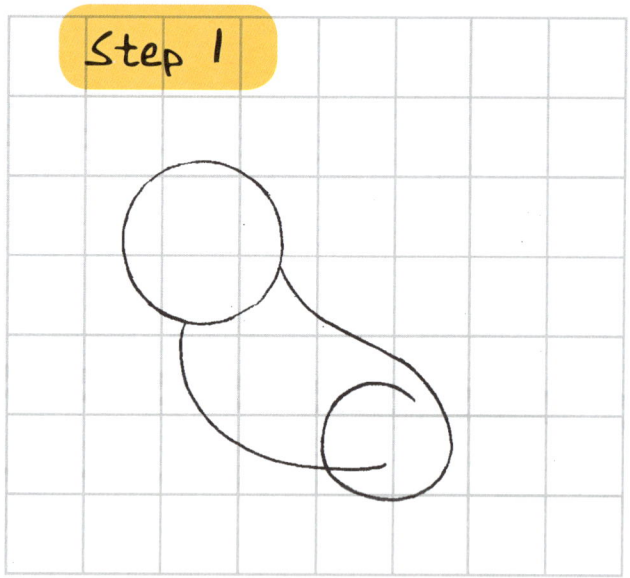

Draw a circle shape for the head. Add the rest of the body as shown.

Step 2

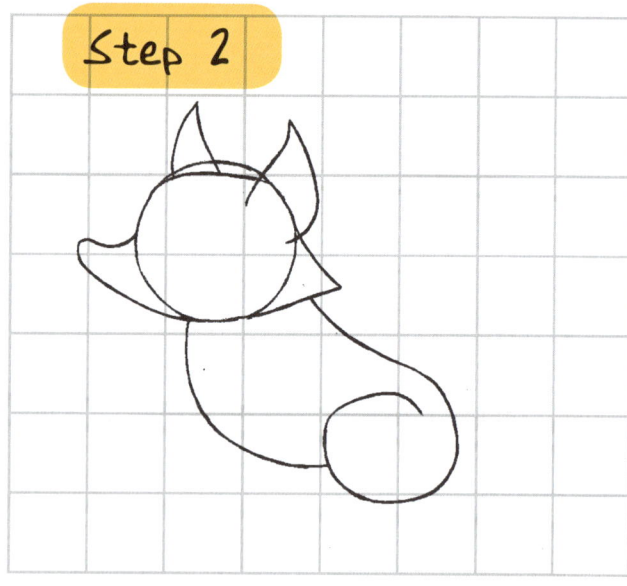

Draw a pointy nose and two pointy ears. Add detail to the face.

Step 3

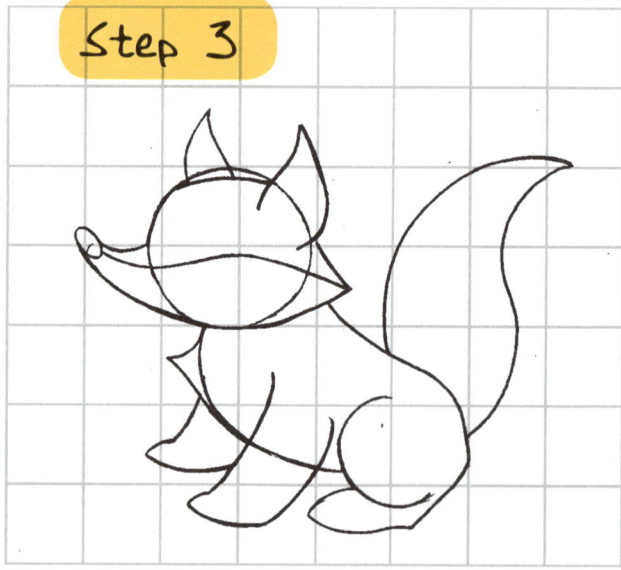

Draw a bush tail and draw the legs. Add a tiny little nose and detail to the face.

Step 4

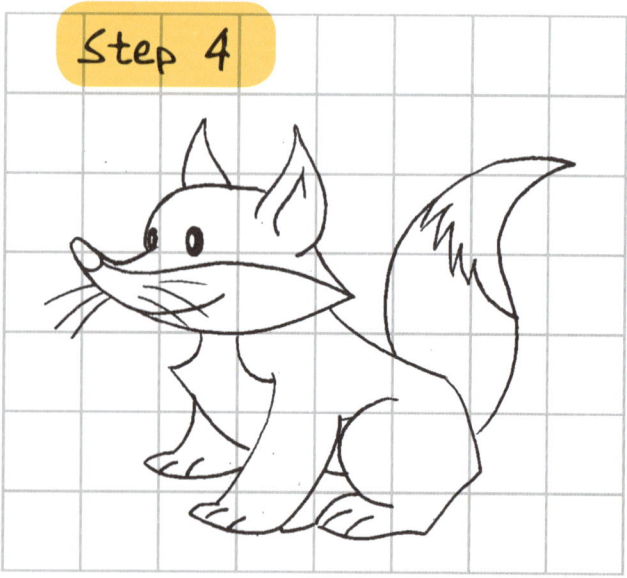

Give the fox eyes and whiskers. Add fur detail to the tail and body.

Place the Sticker

Drawing Tips
Draw from left to right if you are right-handed and vice versa to avoid smudging already drawn and shaded areas.

Colour
like
this

Time to Draw...

Colour in like this!